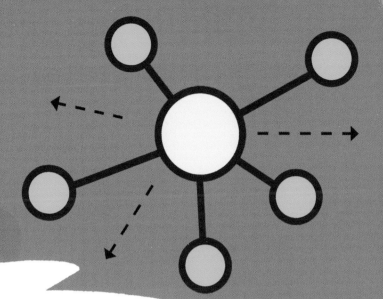

ELEMENTS OF
LIFE

PHOSPHORUS

NANCY DICKMANN

PowerKiDS
press.

Published in 2019 by **The Rosen Publishing Group, Inc.**
29 East 21st Street, New York, NY 10010

Cataloging-in-Publication Data
Names: Dickmann, Nancy.
Title: Phosphorus / Nancy Dickmann.
Description: New York : PowerKids Press, 2019. | Series: Elements of life | Includes glossary and index.
Identifiers: ISBN 9781538347737 (pbk.) | ISBN 9781538347751 (library bound) | ISBN 9781538347744 (6pack)
Subjects: LCSH: Phosphorus--Juvenile literature. | Periodic table of the elements--Juvenile literature.
Classification: LCC QD181.P1 D53 2019 | DDC 546'.712--dc23

Copyright © 2019 Brown Bear Books Ltd

For Brown Bear Books Ltd:
Text and Editor: Nancy Dickmann
Designer and Illustrator: Supriya Sahai
Design Manager: Keith Davis
Picture Manager: Sophie Mortimer
Editorial Director: Lindsey Lowe
Children's Publisher: Anne O'Daly

Concept development: Square and Circus/Brown Bear Books Ltd

Picture Credits
Front Cover: Artwork, Supriya Sahai.
Interior: iStock: Artystarty, 17tr, bleshutterb, 9tr, 29bl, fotokostic, 20-21, 29tr, master1305, 16, Oat Phawat, 14b, PHOTOGraphics, 21tr, red2000, 8, renacal1, 13, 28, SolStock, 24, ssuaphoto, 25br; Public Domain: Alshaer666, 9bl, Derby Museum and Art Gallery/LeisureMuseumsGalleries/Arttreasure/TheAlchymist, 14-15, Endimion17, 11; Science Photo Library: Charles D. Winters, 10; Shutterstock: B Brown, 22-23, Djelen, 25t, Jelloyd, 22l, Linnas, 19tr, NASA Images, 5, Olpo, 12, Positive Studio, 6-7, M Price, 21c.
Key: t=top, b=bottom, c=center, l=left, r=right

Manufactured in the United States of America

CPSIA Compliance Information: Batch CWPK19: For Further Information contact Rosen Publishing, New York, New York at 1-800-237-9932

CONTENTS

ELEMENTS ALL AROUND US

Elements are everywhere. They cannot be broken down into other substances, but they can combine with other elements. Elements make up pebbles, pandas—and you! Oxygen, carbon, hydrogen, nitrogen, phosphorus, and sulfur are the most important elements for life.

ATOMS AND MOLECULES

Elements are made up of atoms, which are too small to see. Atoms are made up of even smaller parts: tiny particles called protons, neutrons, and electrons. Atoms can stick together in a process called bonding. An atom might bond with an atom of the same element, or a different element. When two different elements combine, they form a compound. It might look and react very differently from the original elements.

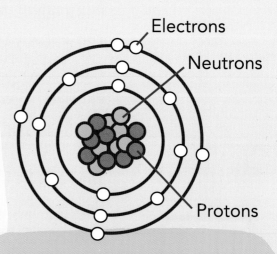

Electrons

Neutrons

Protons

THE PHOSPHORUS ATOM

A phosphorus atom has 15 electrons, 15 protons, and 16 neutrons. Versions with different numbers of neutrons have been made in laboratories.

PHENOMENAL PHOSPHORUS

Phosphorus may not be one of the most common elements in the universe, but it is essential for life. It is found in all living things and it plays an important role in life processes.

Scientists think that phosphorus forms when stars die in explosions called supernovas.

Natural or Not?

There are about 94 elements that are found in nature. Others have been made in laboratories.

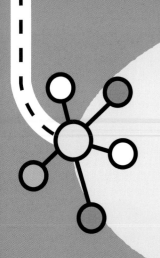

RED AND WHITE

An element can exist in different forms, called allotropes. Different allotropes are all made of the same type of atom, but the atoms are arranged in different ways. The two main allotropes of phosphorus are called red phosphorus and white phosphorus.

WHITE PHOSPHORUS

A molecule of white phosphorus is made up of four phosphorus atoms. Each of the atoms is bonded to each of the other three atoms. This forms a pyramid-like shape called a tetrahedron.

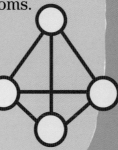

Molecules

Atoms join together to form molecules. A molecule may contain atoms of the same element, or atoms of many different elements. A molecule of a phosphorus allotrope contains only phosphorus atoms.

RED PHOSPHORUS

In red phosphorus, the atoms link together.
Red phosphorus can be produced by heating white
phosphorus. At temperatures of 482°F (250°C) or above,
the bond between two atoms in a tetrahedron is broken.
Those two atoms bond to other tetrahedrons instead,
forming a long chain.

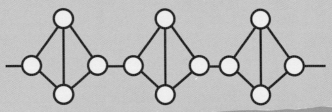

A RAINBOW ELEMENT

Heating or other
processes can produce
other allotropes of
phosphorus, including
black, violet, and scarlet
phosphorus. Just to make
it more complicated, white
phosphorus is sometimes
called yellow phosphorus!

White phosphorus
produces thick clouds
of white smoke when
it burns.

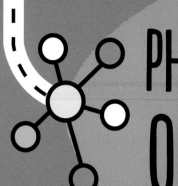

PHYSICAL PROPERTIES OF PHOSPHORUS

Each element is different. Some of an element's properties can be easily measured by using your senses to observe them. These are its physical properties.

Red phosphorus is used in the striking stips on matchboxes. Striking the match against the striking strip makes the match light.

SAME, BUT DIFFERENT

An element's physical properties include its color and odor and how hard it is. Different allotropes of the same element can have very different properties. Red phosphorus and white phosphorus are so different that you might be fooled into thinking they are different elements!

WHITE PHOSPHORUS

STATE: solid at room temperature

MELTING POINT: melts at 111.4°F (44.1°C)

COLOR: white or yellowish

ODOR: smells like matches or garlic

TEXTURE: forms waxy lumps

DISSOLVES IN WATER? No

RED PHOSPHORUS

STATE: solid at room temperature

MELTING POINT: melts at 1,090°F (590°C)

COLOR: dark red, orange, or purple

ODOR: no odor at room temperature

TEXTURE: powder

DISSOLVES IN WATER? No

Black Phos
P ~99.9
0.18 gra

Another allotrope, called black phosphorus, is black and flaky.

CHEMICAL PROPERTIES OF PHOSPHORUS

An element's chemical properties can only be observed when the element reacts with other elements or substances. White phosphorus is so reactive that it is stored underwater.

CHANGING CHEMICALS

When one element combines with another, the atoms of each element are rearranged. This is called a chemical change, and it results in new substances. An element's chemical properties can be measured when a chemical change happens.

White phosphorus is very reactive. It reacts with oxygen in air and bursts into flames.

When white phosphorus reacts slowly with oxygen in the air, it glows in the dark.

ALL ABOUT PHOSPHORUS

Here are a few of the chemical properties of white phosphorus:

It reacts so easily with oxygen that it ignites automatically when exposed to it.

When heated, phosphorus combines with metals to form compounds called phosphides.

Red Phosphorus

Compared to white phosphorus, red phosphorus is very unreactive. It does not easily combine with other elements.

White phosphorus reacts easily with a group of elements called the halogens. These include fluorine, chlorine, bromine, and iodine.

WHERE IS PHOSPHORUS FOUND?

Some elements, such as gold and carbon, are often found on their own, in their free form. Phosphorus, on the other hand, reacts so easily that on Earth it is never found on its own.

PHOSPHORUS COMPOUNDS

Phosphorus on Earth is locked up in compounds, including minerals called phosphates. There are large deposits of phosphorus-rich minerals in the Middle East, China, Russia, North Africa, and the United States. Farmers rely on phosphates as an ingredient of fertilizers.

Apatite is the most common phosphate mineral. It comes in many colors but is usually green.

IN THE CRUST

By weight, phosphorus makes up just under 0.1 percent of Earth's crust. This phosphorus is found in compounds that make up many different minerals.

UNUSUAL SOURCES

Throughout history, humans have gotten phosphorus from other sources, too. Ash from burned bones was an important source. So was human urine and guano (poop of seabirds and bats).

In the 1800s, wars were fought over islands with large guano deposits.

PHOSPHORUS IN SPACE

There is phosphorus in the sun and other stars. Minerals that are rich in phosphorus have been found in some meteorites—space rocks that have landed on Earth. Some scientists believe that meteorites played an important role in building Earth's supply of phosphorus.

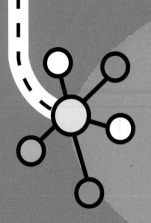

DISCOVERING PHOSPHORUS

Although phosphorus is found in every living thing, scientists didn't discover it until about 350 years ago.

LOOKING FOR GOLD

Hennig Brand was an alchemist working in Germany in the 1660s. Alchemists all had the same goal: they wanted to find a substance called the "philosopher's stone." They believed this stone could turn some metals into gold. They thought it could be used to produce a potion that would allow its drinker to live forever.

Hennig Brand ended up with a glowing substance instead of the philosopher's stone.

Brand collected about 50 buckets of human urine and left them to stand in the sun for several weeks.

The urine began to evaporate, and Brand then boiled it down to a thick syrup.

He heated the syrup and collected the red oil that formed on the top.

Brand let the syrup sit in his cellar until it turned black.

The black substance was mixed with the red oil and heated.

The heating produced glowing fumes that turned into a shining white liquid. Brand had discovered phosphorus.

LIGHT BEARER

Brand was fascinated by the substance he had produced. It hardened into a waxy lump that gave off an eerie glow. Flames appeared as the phosphorus reacted with oxygen in the air. Brand named this new element "phosphorus," which means "light bearer."

PHOSPHORUS IN THE BODY

Without phosphorus, life cannot exist. The small amounts of phosphorus in the human body play a very important role.

THE BIG FOUR

About 96 percent of the human body is made up of just four elements: oxygen, carbon, hydrogen, and nitrogen. Phosphorus comes in sixth place, after calcium, making up about 1 percent of your body's mass.

PHOSPHORUS FOODS

Eating phosphorus-rich foods helps to build strong teeth and bones. Milk and milk products such as cheese are high in phosphorus. Meat, fish, beans, lentils, nuts, and whole grains also have a lot of phosphorus.

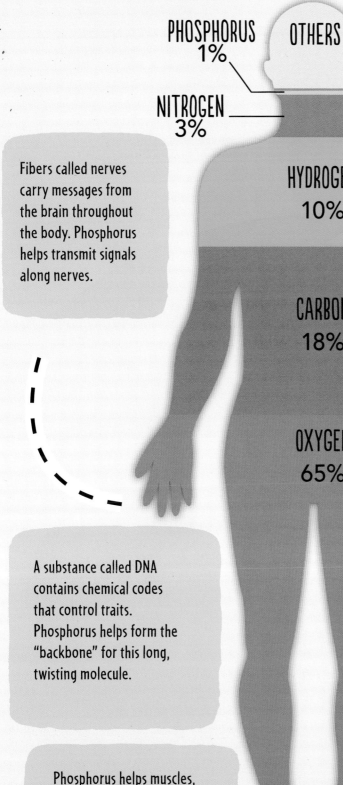

PHOSPHORUS
1%

OTHERS

SULPHUR
0.3%

NITROGEN
3%

HYDROGEN
10%

CARBON
18%

OXYGEN
65%

Fibers called nerves carry messages from the brain throughout the body. Phosphorus helps transmit signals along nerves.

There is phosphorus in every cell of the body, but about 85 percent of the body's phosphorus is found in the bones and teeth. It works with calcium to give these body parts their strength.

A substance called DNA contains chemical codes that control traits. Phosphorus helps form the "backbone" for this long, twisting molecule.

PHOSSY JAW

In the 1800s, phosphorus was widely used for making matches. Workers in match factories breathed in phosphorus fumes. It made their jawbones glow in the dark. Eventually it ate the bone away. Many workers died from this condition, which was called "phossy jaw."

Phosphorus helps muscles, including the heart, contract (squeeze).

PHOSPHORUS AND LIFE

All living things need phosphorus. It moves from the soil to different organisms in a process called the phosphorus cycle.

Wind and rain break down rocks containing phosphorus compounds called phosphates.

Some phosphates are transferred to the soil.

Some phosphates move into the water supply and are carried to the ocean.

ENERGY TRANSFER

Our bodies need energy to do work. The energy we get from food is stored in the form of a molecule called ATP (adenosine triphosphate). This molecule helps to transfer energy from one cell to another. Phosphorus is an important component of ATP.

Plants take in phosphates from the soil.

Plant-eating animals eat the phosphate-rich plants.

RUNNING OUT

A lot of phosphorus ends up in the ocean, where it often sinks to the bottom. This removes it from the phosphorus cycle, and plants and animals can no longer use it. After many years, we will run out of phosphorus sources on Earth's surface.

Meat-eating animals get their phosphates by eating other animals.

When a plant dies, its phosphates return to the soil.

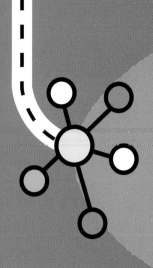

FERTILIZERS

Humans depend on farmers' crops for food. To help their crops grow better, farmers use fertilizers. The key ingredient? Phosphorus!

REPLACING PHOSPHATES

Plants take phosphates out of the soil. In a natural setting, when plants die, they break down and their nutrients are returned to the soil. But when farmers harvest crops, they take the plants away. No nutrients are returned to the soil. To grow the next crop, farmers add fertilizer. It contains phosphates and other nutrients that plants need.

Ancient Fertilizer

Farmers have been using fertilizers for thousands of years. The earliest fertilizer was animal manure. Early farmers also used ground bone, ash, and guano.

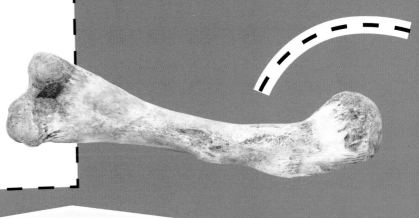

Fertilizers containing phosphorus help farmers grow healthy crops.

SYNTHETIC FERTILIZERS

In the 1830s, the English chemist John Bennet Lawes experimented with different fertilizers, testing them on potted plants and in the fields. In 1842 he developed a process for manufacturing fertilizer. He soon opened a factory that used this process, treating phosphate-rich rocks with sulfuric acid, to manufacture large amounts of fertilizer.

PHOSPHATE PROBLEMS

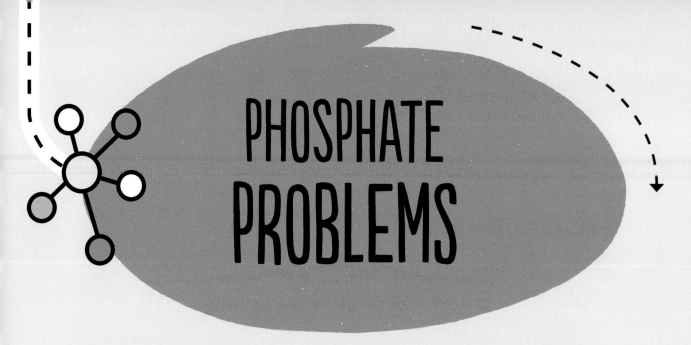

Fertilizers have changed the way we farm, making it possible to feed the Earth's growing population. But their use also has a downside.

TOO MUCH PHOSPHORUS

Phosphates in fertilizer can easily end up in rivers, streams, and lakes. It can cause serious changes in these bodies of water, making conditions difficult for the plants and animals that live there.

Farmers put phosphate fertilizers on their fields.

When it rains, some fertilizer is washed away. It ends up in rivers and streams.

Nutrients in the fertilizer are good for algae and other plants. These plants grow rapidly.

PHOSPHATE MINING

Mining phosphate rock damages the landscape. Giant shovels strip away the earth to reach the phosphate-rich rocks below. Large amounts of water are used to separate out the phosphate from the other materials.

When algae covers the surface, less sunlight can get through. Plants below the surface die if they don't get enough sunlight.

Plants produce oxygen. If they die, there will be less oxygen in the water.

Mining phosphates often leaves huge holes in the ground.

Dead plants are broken down by bacteria, which use up even more of the oxygen in the water.

If there is not enough oxygen, fish and other water animals will die.

USING PHOSPHORUS

Although phosphorus is not one of Earth's most common elements, it is extremely useful. We use phosphorus and phosphorus compounds in many ways.

Phosphoric acid is used to make baking powder and some soft drinks.

Phosphorus is used in the production of steel and the smelting of copper.

By far, the biggest use of phosphorus is in the production of fertilizers. These fertilizers make it possible for farmers to feed the world.

White phosphorus burns very easily. It is used in flares and in bombs and grenades that are designed to start fires.

White phosphorus gives off thick smoke when it burns. It is used in smoke grenades, which help armed forces mask the movement of soldiers or vehicles.

Phosphates were often used in detergents, but their use is being phased out. These detergents cause the same problems in bodies of water as fertilizers do.

THE PERIODIC TABLE

All the elements are organized into a chart called the periodic table. It groups together elements with similar properties. Each square gives information about a particular element.

A Good Idea!

The periodic table was developed in the 1860s by a Russian chemist named Dmitri Mendeleev. He left gaps that were later filled in with new elements, as they were discovered.

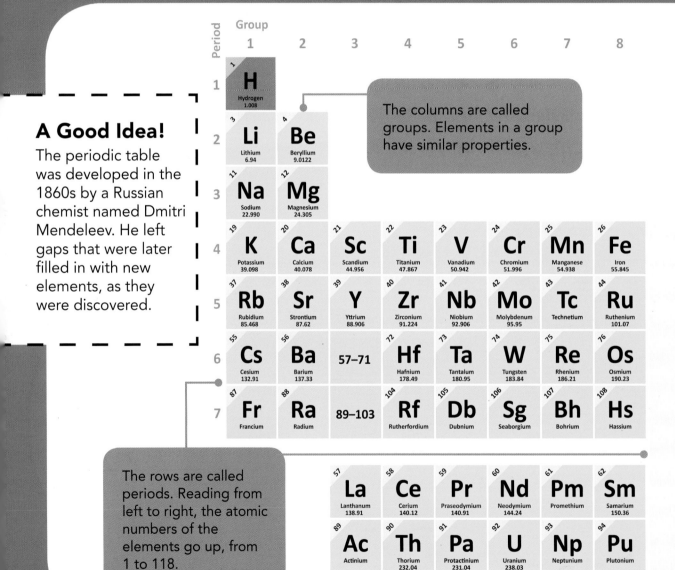

The columns are called groups. Elements in a group have similar properties.

The rows are called periods. Reading from left to right, the atomic numbers of the elements go up, from 1 to 118.

Every element has an atomic number. It shows how many protons are in each of its atoms. The atomic number for phosphorus is 15.

The chemical symbol is one or two letters, often an abbreviation of the element's name. It is the same in all languages.

15

P

Phosphorus
30.974

Each square shows the element's name. Different languages use different names.

A number shows the element's atomic weight. It is an average of the number of protons and neutrons in the different isotopes of an element.

9	10	11	12	13	14	15	16	17	18

Metalloids (semimetals)

Non–metals

Metals

2
He
Helium
4.0026

5
B
Boron
10.81

6
C
Carbon
12.011

7
N
Nitrogen
14.007

8
O
Oxygen
15.999

9
F
Fluorine
18.998

10
Ne
Neon
20.180

13
Al
Aluminum
26.982

14
Si
Silicon
28.085

15
P
Phosphorus
30.974

16
S
Sulfur
32.06

17
Cl
Chlorine
35.45

18
Ar
Argon
39.948

27
Co
Cobalt
58.933

28
Ni
Nickel
58.693

29
Cu
Copper
63.546

30
Zn
Zinc
65.38

31
Ga
Gallium
69.723

32
Ge
Germanium
72.630

33
As
Arsenic
74.922

34
Se
Selenium
78.971

35
Br
Bromine
79.904

36
Kr
Krypton
83.798

45
Rh
Rhodium
102.91

46
Pd
Palladium
106.42

47
Ag
Silver
107.87

48
Cd
Cadmium
112.41

49
In
Indium
114.82

50
Sn
Tin
118.71

51
Sb
Antimony
121.76

52
Te
Tellurium
127.60

53
I
Iodine
126.90

54
Xe
Xenon
131.29

77
Ir
Iridium
192.22

78
Pt
Platinum
195.08

79
Au
Gold
196.97

80
Hg
Mercury
200.59

81
Tl
Thallium
204.38

82
Pb
Lead
207.2

83
Bi
Bismuth
208.98

84
Po
Polonium

85
At
Astatine

86
Rn
Radon

109
Mt
Meitnerium

110
Ds
Darmstadtium

111
Rg
Roentgenium

112
Cn
Copernicium

113
Nh
Nihonium

114
Fl
Flerovium

115
Mc
Moscovium

116
Lv
Livermorium

117
Ts
Tennessine

118
Og
Oganesson

63
Eu
Europium
151.96

64
Gd
Gadolinium
157.25

65
Tb
Terbium
158.93

66
Dy
Dysprosium
162.50

67
Ho
Holmium
164.93

68
Er
Erbium
167.26

69
Tm
Thulium
168.93

70
Yb
Ytterbium
173.05

71
Lu
Lutetium
174.97

Lanthanide elements

95
Am
Americium

96
Cm
Curium

97
Bk
Berkelium

98
Cf
Californium

99
Es
Einsteinium

100
Fm
Fermium

101
Md
Mendelevium

102
No
Nobelium

103
Lr
Lawrencium

Actinide elements

QUIZ

Try this quiz and test your knowledge of phosphorus and elements! The answers are on page 32.

1

What is a compound?

a. an old-fashioned unit for measuring weight
b. a substance formed when two or more elements combine
c. a flashy but dangerous dance move

2

What do red phosphorus and white phosphorus have in common?

a. they are made up purely of phosphorus atoms
b. they like long walks on the beach
c. they both form pale, waxy lumps

3

What does white phosphorus smell like?

a. rotten eggs
b. peppermint
c. matches or garlic

4

What is guano?

a. a delicious dip made from avocados
b. the phosphate-rich poop of seabirds and bats
c. a compound formed from gold and carbon

5

How did Hennig Brand isolate pure phosphorus?

a. he boiled down buckets of human urine
b. he mixed rainwater with ground-up rock
c. it was an accident; he was trying to cook soup

6

Why do farmers use phosphate fertilizers?

a. because they are less smelly than using manure
b. to make their vegetables more brightly colored
c. to replace the phosphorus that their crops take out of the soil

7

What did phosphorus fumes do to some workers in match factories?

a. made them go blind
b. made their jawbones glow and eventually rot away
c. made them have really weird dreams

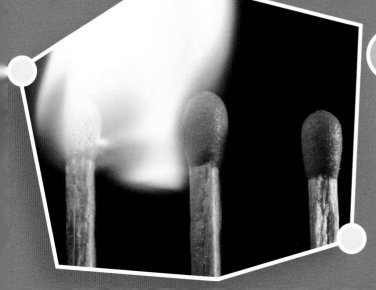

8

Which type of phosphorus is in the striking strip on a box of matches?

a. red phosphorus
b. white phosphorus
c. turquoise phosphorus

GLOSSARY

acid a substance with a low pH that usually has a sour taste and eats away other materials

alchemist person from long ago who tried to find a way to turn metals into gold

allotropes different forms of the same element. One allotrope of an element has the atoms arranged in a different pattern than other allotropes of the same element.

atom the smallest possible unit of a chemical element. Atoms are the basis of all matter in the universe.

bacteria tiny living things that can cause infection but that can also be useful, such as by breaking down dead matter

bond to form a link with other atoms, either of the same element or of a different element

cell the smallest unit of life. All plants and animals are made of cells.

chemical change change that occurs when one substance reacts with another to form a new substance

chemical property characteristic of a material that can be observed during or after a chemical reaction

compound substance made of two or more different elements bonded together

crust the hard, outermost layer of Earth

electron a tiny particle with a negative charge that moves outside the nucleus of an atom

element a substance that cannot be broken down or separated into other substances

energy the ability to do work. Energy can take many different forms.

evaporate to turn from a liquid into a gas

fertilizer substance that farmers put on fields to help crops grow better

gas form of matter that is neither liquid or solid

guano the solid waste of seabirds and bats, which can be used as a fertilizer

ignite to catch fire

isotopes different forms of the same element. One isotope of an element has a different number of neutrons than other isotopes of the same element.

liquid form of matter that is neither a solid nor a gas, and flows when it is poured

mass the total amount of matter in an object or space

molecule the smallest unit of a substance that has all the properties of that substance. A molecule can be made up of a single atom, or a group of atoms

neutron a particle in the nucleus of an atom with no charge

phosphates compounds formed from phosphorus and oxygen, which are necessary for life

physical property characteristic of a material that can be observed without changing the material

proton a positively charged particle in the nucleus of an atom

react to undergo a chemical change when combined with another substance

tetrahedron 3D shape with four corners and four triangular faces arranged in a pyramid shape

FURTHER RESOURCES

BOOKS

Arbuthnott, Gill. *Your Guide to the Periodic Table.* New York, NY: Crabtree Publishing Company, 2016.

Callery, Sean, and Miranda Smith. *Periodic Table.* New York, NY: Scholastic Nonfiction, 2017.

Carmichael, L.E. *How Can We Reduce Agricultural Pollution?* Minneapolis, MN: Lerner Publications, 2016.

Linde, Barbara. *Strip Mining.* New York, NY: Gareth Stevens Publishing, 2014.

Slingerland, Janet. *Explore Atoms and Molecules!* White River Junction, VT: Nomad Press, 2017.

Stefoff, Rebecca. *Alchemy and Chemistry.* New York, NY: Cavendish Square Publishing, 2014.

WEBSITES

This website explains more about phosphorus:
www.ducksters.com/science/chemistry/phosphorus.php

Go here for amazing facts about phosphorus:
www.livescience.com/28932-phosphorus.html

Learn about all the elements using this interactive periodic table:
www.rsc.org/periodic-table/

Visit this website to find out how phosphorus is used.
sciencestruck.com/phosphorus-uses

INDEX

Quiz answers
1. b; 2. a; 3. c; 4. b; 5. a;
6. c; 7. b; 8. a